FAITH & FRIENDS™

Bridget's Blog

Faith & Friends™

Bridget's Blog

Written by Wendy Witherow
Illustrations by Kelly Pulley

MCP
Mission City Press
Bringing Faith to Life™

Bridget's Blog

Published by Mission City Press, Inc.

Cover and Interior Art: Kelly Pulley
Typesetting: Bob Bubnis, BookSetters

For more information, write to Mission City Press at 202 Second Avenue South, Franklin, Tennessee 37064, or visit our Web Site at:

www.faithandfriends.com

Library of Congress Catalog Card Number: 2007922299
Witherow, Wendy

ISBN-13: 978-1-934306-09-3

Printed in the United States of America
1 2 3 4 5 6 7 8 — 11 10 09 08 07

Dedication

To William John Davis—for the polka-dotted
elephants that sparked imagination.
And to Myrna Caroline Davis—for always believing.

Chapter One

Twilight was settling upon the small town of Wishing, Iowa. A sprinkling of gleaming, summer stars had begun to peek through the fading purple clouds. Bridget stood at her bedroom window and looked out past her backyard toward the endless rows of cornfields next to their property. Her neighbor's huge grain silo was silhouetted on the horizon. Hundreds of fireflies blinked and glowed, and the faint song of a cricket could be heard.

"Whatcha doing, Bridgey?" asked little seven-year-old Allison. She stood at the door of her big sister's bedroom. Her large, hazel eyes curiously studied Bridget.

"I'm just thinking," Bridget said dreamily.

Allison padded over to Bridget and leaned against her. Bridget wrapped her arm around her sister's small shoulders.

"Whatcha thinking about?" asked Allison.

A cool breeze slipped through the screen and swept over them.

Bridget sighed happily. "I was imagining that the Thompsons' grain silo was really a huge skyscraper in New York City, and that the corn stalks were the city folks hustling and bustling about."

"You're silly, Bridgey," Allison said through a yawn.

"You're too young to understand, Ali," Bridget replied, and then pointed to a colorful poster of Times Square. "It's been my lifelong dream to live in New York City and be someone important—like a Broadway performer or a famous writer. This summer I'll finally get to go there when I visit Aunt Faith. I can't wait! Isn't the city just fabulous? All the people are *so* beautiful."

But something else caught Allison's attention— something just as colorful. "I think *she's* beautiful," Allison said, pointing to a doll that was perched on the windowsill. The doll seemed to be enjoying the view. "Who is she?" Ali asked, picking up the doll.

"That's what I've been wondering," Bridget said. Allison gave Bridget a questioning look.

"She's my new friend," Bridget explained. "Mom got her for me today when she got you your new stuffed bunny. I'm going to write a short story about her. But first I have to give her a name."

"I like her freckles and her long, shiny hair," Allison said. "Her clothes are pretty too."

Bridget agreed with her little sister and admired the doll's colorful outfit. "Maybe I'll find clothes like this on 5th Avenue," Bridget said with excitement.

Allison shrugged and handed the doll back to her sister. "What's 5th Avenue?" she asked.

"They say it's only *the most* fashionable street for shopping in all of New York. I sure hope Auntie Faith takes me there."

Allison yawned. "Well, your doll sure is pretty. Good night, Bridgey."

"Sweet dreams," Bridget said as Allison left the room.

Bridget took the doll and looked deeply into her soft, blue eyes. "Who *are* you?" she whispered. The doll's kind face smiled back at her.

There's a special twinkle in her eyes, Bridget thought. *Her eyes shine like stars . . .*

Bridget was suddenly reminded of a Scripture verse from her morning devotional book. She went to her nightstand and picked up the book.

"Here it is! Daniel 12:3: 'Those who are wise will shine like the brightness of the heavens, and those who lead many to righteousness, like the stars for ever and ever.'"

She climbed into her canopied bed and made herself comfortable beneath a purple blanket.

Wise . . . lead many to righteousness . . . like the stars . . .

Bridget sat the doll next to her atop a brightly embroidered pillow with pink feather trim. The colorful doll seemed right at home.

"You look smart," Bridget said thoughtfully, "and sweet and inspiring. You've got great style, too. I'll bet lots of girls would want to be *your* friend."

She picked up the doll. "I like your hair the best. It looks a lot like mine," Bridget said as she stroked the doll's long, strawberry blonde hair.

Bridget's thoughts turned to her uneasiness about starting the sixth grade at the end of the summer. "I wonder if the older kids will like me," she said to the doll. "The seventh and eighth grade girls seem to always look great and know exactly what to wear."

Bridget ran her fingers through her own long hair. "Maybe they'll like my hair. Will they think I've got great style?" Bridget paused. "Could I ever be inspiring to anyone?"

Bridget rolled over and placed the doll on the nightstand next to the alarm clock. "I have plenty of time to worry about all of that. Besides, I know Auntie Faith will help me find some great clothes when I'm in New York City. For now I should just work on finding you a name," she told her new doll.

"Good night, starry-eyes," Bridget said sleepily as she clicked off the lamp.

Thank You for this day, Heavenly Father. Please bless my Mom and Dad and watch over Ali. And be with Auntie Faith and Tina and the rest of my family and friends. And please help me figure out a name for my doll.

With lingering thoughts of names and New York City, Bridget fell fast asleep.

 # Chapter Two

Bridget's Blog

Hello friends! To kick off the opening of our new family web site that Dad created, I've decided to start a blog to tell all about my summer happenings (a blog is a web log, in case you didn't know. It's kinda like an online diary). So here it is—my first ever blog entry!

To begin with, it's officially the first day of summer. Whew! I made it through the fifth grade! To celebrate, my mom took me to the Nervous Squirrel Cafe for my first ever "triple-nut-chocolate-mint-frozen-swirrelly-squirrelly"! Talk about a chocolate overload!

In other news, Mrs. Hirsch (my new sixth grade teacher) gave us a creative writing assignment to complete over the summer for extra credit. We can choose any subject to write about. I'm going to try and pen a short story inspired by my new doll. Maybe it'll help launch my writing career!

I'm really keyed up about my summer—mostly because I'm going to New York City!!! All my life I've dreamed about seeing the Big Apple. I can't wait to walk along 5th Avenue and gaze up at the skyscrapers!

I have a confession to make: All of this summer excitement can't hide the fact that I'm already really nervous about starting middle school in the fall! Everybody seems so grown up and knows exactly what to do and what to say, and especially what to wear! I have no idea what the sixth grade will be like. Will I fit in? (Please, please, please pray for me.) Since this blog is F.Y.E.O.—for your eyes only—I can be the *real* me.

Check out my blog often so we can stay connected and I'll keep you posted on all of our family's latest adventures.

With a final click on the keyboard, Bridget sat back and smiled with satisfaction. "It's official, Mom! I just started my very first blog. Wanna see?"

"Of course," said Sandra Rhodes, Bridget's mom, as she stepped away from a steaming pot of spaghetti and walked over to the family laptop. "Very nice," Mrs. Rhodes said as she browsed the page. "I'm glad you shared your heart with us," she added, giving Bridget a hug.

"I double checked the filter and privacy settings on the blog, too," Bridget said. "Only family members and a couple of my friends can read it."

Mrs. Rhodes nodded her approval. "Very good. You're turning into quite the tech-head, my dear."

"What can I say? It's the wave of the future," Bridget said with dramatic flair.

Mrs. Rhodes smiled. "I suppose so. But right now I need you to log in to kitchen duty and help set the table."

"Cute, Mom."

"I'm up on my cyber lingo! I'm not *that* old," Mrs. Rhodes said with a snicker.

Bridget giggled as she pulled together the dinner plates, glasses, napkins, and silverware and began setting the kitchen table.

"Have you picked a name for your doll yet?" her mom asked.

Bridget folded a napkin and squinted her nose. "I've got some ideas and I've been praying about it, but I was hoping to spend some time online looking up names. It's such a *big* decision. I want something really special."

"Names are important," her mom agreed. "Your dad and I studied hundreds of names before settling on yours."

"It means 'strong,' doesn't it?" Bridget asked.

"Yes, that's right. Our prayer was that you would be strong in the Lord all your days."

" 'Be strong in the Lord and in his mighty power,' " Bridget quoted from Ephesians 6. "That's the verse that inspired you and Dad to name me *Bridget*."

"And it's still our prayer for you, darling," her mom said tenderly.

"It's my prayer for me, too," Bridget replied, smiling.

"By the way, if you're worried about fitting in when school starts," Mrs. Rhodes said, "the best way to fit in is to simply be yourself and let God's love shine through you. You will fit in just fine."

"Keep reminding me of that, Mom!" Bridget said with a sigh.

Bridget finished setting the table and walked to the stove. "You know," she said thoughtfully as she stirred the spaghetti sauce, "now that I think about it, last night I may have found a verse to inspire my doll's name."

"Wonderful! There are names in the Bible you might consider too," said her mom.

"Mmmm. I smell garlic! My stomach's growling!" Michael Rhodes came striding into the kitchen. He slid his briefcase into the corner with practiced finesse. "What more could a man ask for after a long day at the office—two beautiful ladies and the delicious smell of garlic bread."

"Welcome home, my dear. Your timing is perfect. We're just about ready to eat—"

"Dad! You've *got* to see the blog I created on our family web site!" Bridget said emphatically. She left her post at the spaghetti sauce and was leading him to the computer when her mom interrupted.

"Wait a minute! Supper first, okay? Then you can unveil your newly created cyber masterpiece. Do you mind fetching your sister? She's in the backyard."

"All right, Mom. But Dad, you're gonna love it!" Bridget breezed past her dad and headed for the back door.

Michael and Sandra Rhodes heard the screen door slam, followed by a shrill, "A-l-l-i-s-o-n! Time to eat!" They looked at each other with wry smiles.

"Summer is here," Sandra said with laughter in her voice.

Chapter Three

Bridget's Blog

Start Spreading the News!!!

Do you want the good news first, or the even better news first??? (I know—it's only the second week of summer and already life is like a bowlful of ~~cherries!~~ I mean apples . . .)

First: Today Mom booked our flights to New York City! She called Auntie Faith and everything is set for our weekend in the BIG APPLE. Auntie Faith is getting us tickets to a Broadway musical. She's promised to show us as much of the city as is humanly possible in three days. We leave in two months, just days before school starts. How can I wait two whole months? I must start packing immediately. . . . (If my bf Tina is out there reading this, can you call me ASAP? I'd really like your help with the packing and planning. Oh, and can I please borrow your patchwork denim skirt for my big debut on Broadway??? I so wish you were coming with me!!!)

Second: I'm off to a great start on the story I'm writing. The biggest problem so far has been finding the perfect name for my doll, who represents the main character. I want her name to reflect the kind of person she would be. So I did what every great author does—research! With Mom's help I found a web site that lists hundreds of names and their meanings. I used a personality profile sheet I found online to help me dream up her character and interests. I even found a Scripture verse, Daniel 12:3, which helped inspire her name:

> "Those who are wise will shine like the brightness of the heavens, and those who lead many to righteousness, like the stars for ever and ever."

So with no further ado, I hereby unveil the coolest name ever! Drum roll, please!

The new name of my doll is:

"Star Arianna"

Star comes from the name Esther. Esther was a wise queen who helped save the lives of the Israelites. She was brave and inspiring and she loved God.

Arianna means "holy," and besides that, it sounds really cool!

Together, Star Arianna is simply the perfect name for my doll. (Thanks, God!) She's the kind of person I want to be, too.

World, meet Star...Star, meet the world!

Chapter Four

I can't believe you are really going to New York City!" Tina Davies exclaimed as she leaned closer to her best friend. The girls peered at each other from behind two jumbo fresh fruit smoothies. They sat at a little table in the window of the downtown coffee shop, the Nervous Squirrel, while Mrs. Rhodes ran a few errands. Tina's older sister, Amy, worked behind the counter and promised to keep an eye on them. Tina took a long sip through her straw, and her glasses slid to the tip of her nose.

Bridget couldn't hide a giggle. "You still aren't used to your new glasses, huh?" she asked.

"I think they're too big—do you think they're too big?" Tina asked in a rush of words. She pushed the glasses back in place with one swift motion and then struck a dramatic pose. Her straight black hair swished—then her glasses slid right back down to the tip of her nose. The girls erupted in laughter before being shushed by a man reading a newspaper.

"I like the style of the frames," Bridget said in a hushed tone. "They suit your brown eyes. But maybe they are a bit too big."

"I'll have to get them adjusted," Tina said. Then she took another sip of her delicious drink. "Now, back to New York City. Tell me all about it!"

Bridget smiled. "Aunt Faith has lived there for six months now. She says her apartment is the size of a matchbox and we'll be like sardines." The girls giggled quietly. "She works for a publishing company. She helps find great writers. Isn't that so cool?" Tina nodded.

"Anyhow, I'm hoping she'll be able to give me some writing tips while I'm there," said Bridget.

"How is your story about Star Arianna coming along?" asked Tina. "I read your blog."

"So far, so good," Bridget replied. "But writing a story isn't as easy as I first thought," Bridget added. "I have her profile mostly all filled out. It's really fun to make up her favorite color and foods, and what her personality is like. But thinking up a story is a little different."

"Maybe I can help," Tina suggested.

"What a great idea!" said Bridget, grabbing her backpack and pulling out Star Arianna along with a notebook and pen.

The girls began to brainstorm. There was a lot of giggling and ideas exchanged, and more giggling, but they could not come up with a really good idea. Pages of notes later, they stopped.

"All of this work and nothing seems quite right," Bridget said. "But thanks for helping me try."

"Don't give up, Bridget. An idea will come to you. Look, there's your mom. I guess it's time to go."

As Bridget gathered her things she prayed a silent prayer: *Lord, I really want to write something fun and exciting about Star. You led me to such a wonderful name. Now will You help me with a good story?*

"Girls, are you ready to go?" Mrs. Rhodes bustled into the coffee shop. Her cheeks were freckled and rosy from the summer sun. She slipped her sunglasses to the top of her head, revealing bright, hazel eyes like Bridget's and Allison's. "I've got a trunkload of groceries that need to be put away and a soon-to-be-hungry family to feed. Plus, we need to take Tina home and then pick up your sister from swimming lessons, and somewhere in between I'd like to work in the garden, and—"

"Maybe I should write an exposé about a day in the life of a mom," Bridget stated, and the girls laughed all the way out the door.

"You have no idea," Mrs. Rhodes called after them.

Chapter Five

Bridget's Blog

Hello faithful readers!

I think you will really like this week's blog. It's interactive! I'm conducting a survey and I'd like to hear from you. But first let me explain the "how" and "why" of my survey.

My bf Tina said something yesterday at the Nervous Squirrel that I've been thinking about. (Hi Tina, if you're reading this.) We were brainstorming ideas for Star's story when she said, "Maybe you could write about a great challenge that Star would have to overcome." All last night I was thinking about great challenges.

I began to wonder what you, my friends and family, would find challenging. Would it be something physical, like climbing Mount Everest? Or maybe standing up against a bully? Or scoring well on a big test?

My Aunt Faith, who grew up in our beloved small town of just over 8,000 people, recently moved to New York City—a "town" of over 8 million people! Maybe some of you would find that challenging. (I think it would be a challenge to fit all those people in one place. I guess I'll see it for myself soon enough!)

I've had some challenges of my own this year: Mr. Williams' history tests really forced me to study extra hard. And the kickball tournament on the last day of school was physically challenging. I had to really push myself to stay in the game.

I've got some challenges ahead of me, too. I've been thinking about them a lot lately. I'm really excited about going to middle school in the fall, but as I've said, I'm also nervous. There will be older kids and the school is much bigger. I sure hope I'll fit in with the seventh and eighth graders. Those older girls are so stylish and seem to have it all together. I don't know if I could ever fit in with them. I'm just glad I have Tina as my best friend. We'll get through it together, I'm sure!

Getting up in front of people makes me uneasy, too. Like auditioning for the sixth grade choir. I know it will be very scary. What if I'm so nervous that I won't be able to sing a single note?

Relying on my favorite Scripture verse has helped me with challenges. It is Ephesians 6: "Be strong in the Lord and in his mighty power." When you send me your challenges, please send in your favorite Scripture verse, too (or any other tips that have been helpful when you've faced a challenge).

To help get you started, I looked up the word "challenge" in the dictionary, and here's what it said: "A test of one's abilities or resources in a demanding but stimulating undertaking."

Now it's time for me to hear from you. Please email me some of the greatest challenges you have ever faced, or send me one that you think would be hard. Don't forget to include a Bible verse or other tips that have helped you overcome a challenge. I'm hoping that your experiences and thoughts will help spark a really good idea for Star's story.

The challenge has been set!

Bridget—signing off.

 Chapter
Six

A few days later, Bridget stood in the
bathroom brushing her long, golden
brown hair. "Maybe I'll braid my hair today like Aunt
Faith showed me," she said. She began sectioning off
her hair and braiding it with ease. Star Arianna sat on
the edge of the sink smiling back at her.

"My hair's almost as long as yours, Star," Bridget
said to the doll. "I've been growing my hair long since
the fourth grade. Aunt Faith inspired me. I can't wait
for you to meet her. She's got the longest, prettiest
hair I've ever seen—"

"B-r-i-d-g-e-y!"

Bridget jumped, startled by the shout, and nearly
let go of the braid. Her round, hazel eyes darted

toward the door where her sister was peeking around the corner. "Allison! You surprised me. I thought everyone was downstairs."

"We are. Daddy sent me to get you. Breakfast is ready. You'd better hurry. He said he's really hungry and might eat it all."

"I just need to finish this last little bit . . . there, I'm done."

"Your hair sure has gotten long," Allison commented. "Will you braid mine, too?"

"Sure. Here—it will only take a minute or two."

Allison stood very still while Bridget's hands worked swiftly through Allison's shoulder-length locks.

"Are you going to grow your hair as long as Star's?" Ali asked, picking up the doll.

"I'm so close now," Bridget replied, "maybe in a few more months it'll be even longer than hers."

"You'd have the longest hair in the sixth grade," Allison remarked. "Probably in the whole middle school!"

Bridget pondered that statement. "I've seen some of the popular seventh and eighth grade girls. They have long and gorgeous hair," Bridget said reluctantly.

"But Tina says you have the *prettiest* hair in your class," Allison reminded her.

Bridget glanced at herself in the mirror. *I do love my long hair,* she admitted to herself. *I plan to have the longest hair in my class this year. By the end of summer it should be a few inches longer and I can reach that goal. Just think of all the styles I could do with it! I bet I could look just as fashionable as those older girls do.*

Bridget finished the braid. "There, Ali. You're all done. It looks great. We'd better get downstairs."

The girls headed to the kitchen where a grand breakfast awaited them. It was an exciting Saturday. The Rhodes family was headed to Pierce's Pike—an amusement park two hours away—for a day of roller coasters and water rides. The best part was that Tina was joining them.

After breakfast, Mr. Rhodes loaded the mini-van with a cooler full of bottled waters, sandwiches, and other munchies while the girls packed towels, sunblock lotion, and an extra change of clothes. "Load 'em up!" hollered Mr. Rhodes. "We don't want to keep Tina and Pierce's Pike waiting!"

"What a day!" A chorus of weary giggles filled the Rhodes family's minivan. Tina, Bridget, and Allison were slumped in their seats wearing tired smiles. Despite the sunblock, Bridget's and Allison's beige complexions were much tanner and slightly freckled, while Tina's porcelain skin was pink from the sun.

"Thanks so much for inviting me," Tina said to everyone. "I had a blast!"

"Are you kidding me?" Bridget declared. "I wouldn't have wanted to go without you. You make everything so much fun!"

After they discussed their favorite rides, Tina turned her attention to a sleepy Bridget. "I read your blog about challenges the other day. I'm posting my response tomorrow," Tina said with a hint of mystery.

"Now I'm curious," said Bridget.

Tina giggled. "You'll have to wait. But let's just say that today I faced a challenge—and I won!"

 Chapter
Seven

Bridget's Blog

To kick off this week's blog, I'd like to thank everyone for their contributions to my "challenge" post. I received some awesome answers. Now I have plenty of ideas for Star's story. Thank you!!! Here are some of the responses I received—enjoy!

DAD'S CHALLENGE: My job as district superintendent of the county school system presents me with challenges each week. I enjoy most of them. They cause me to search out creative solutions. I've found that saying a prayer for guidance before problem-solving is of great help. Training for the Boston Marathon (a 26-mile race) would be very challenging and would prove difficult for me.

MOM'S CHALLENGE: This winter I was elected president of the garden club. I was thrilled with the honor, but was unsure if I could lead the club and keep up with my other responsibilities. I had to make some adjustments to my schedule, but the challenge has been rewarding. I think it would be an enormous feat to be head horticulturist at the White House. I admire and respect the work it takes to keep the gardens and lawn at the White House looking so beautiful. Isaiah 26:3 is a source of strength to me: "You will keep in perfect peace him whose mind is steadfast, because he trusts in you."

AUNTIE FAITH'S CHALLENGE: Moving to NYC was certainly a challenge—but a challenge that I loved and still thrive on each day that I'm here. Like Bridget, the thought of getting up in front of people is so frightening. I think public speaking would be one of the greatest challenges I'd ever have to face. Philippians 4:13 has been a Scripture that helps me when I'm in a tough spot: "I can do everything through him who gives me strength."

TINA'S CHALLENGE: I am terrified of a ride at Pierce's Pike called The Drop-Off. This ride lifts you up 24 stories high and then plunges you down at the speed of nearly 60 mph! I've never ridden it even though I've visited Pierce's Pike several times. But this weekend I overcame my fear! It was a h-u-g-e challenge for me. I was really nervous. I think an even greater challenge would be to jump out of an airplane with a parachute. I certainly never plan on doing that! I have not thought about having a special Bible verse to help me when I'm faced with a challenge, but now I'm "challenged" to find one! Thanks, Bridg!

GRANDMA & GRANDPA RHODES' CHALLENGE: Our greatest joy and greatest challenge has been 40 years of marriage. At our age there is little we consider too challenging, as we have learned to face life's challenges with confidence in the Lord. Our favorite verse is from Matthew 19:26: "With man this is impossible, but with God all things are possible."

EMILY D.'S CHALLENGE: Hi Bridget! I like your blog! I saw Tina at church and she told me about it. Let's hang out sometime before school starts. I'll call you. Now, about challenges . . . mine is the sixth grade volleyball tryouts. I'm nervous about it, but I've been practicing my bumps and spikes! I like the verse from 1 Corinthians 9:24: "Do you not know that in a race all the runners run, but only one gets the prize? Run in such a way as to get the prize." The tryouts will be hard, but I'll give it my best shot!

 Chapter
Eight

Once upon a time . . .

No! Totally cheesy!

It was a dark and stormy night . . .

That doesn't fit at all!

In the beginning . . .

That's been used before, too! Come on, Bridget! Think! Just think. Close your eyes and it will come to you. Think about her name . . . think about her personality . . . think about her—you know her so well. She's your new best friend. Just write what is in your heart—write what is in her heart!

One bright spotlight pooled in the center of a dark, empty stage.

Hmmm ... that's not too bad ...

Behind the curtain, dozens of young singers and actors dressed in black paced silently. The tension backstage was almost unbearable, and many a brow was damp from nervous energy.

Keep going! You're on to something ...

From a break in the curtain, some took turns peeking out into the dark auditorium. Four silhouettes could be seen sitting in the middle of the front row, scribbling notes and whispering to one another. All was quiet as the group awaited announcement of the next name.

At least that's what I imagine it would be like . . . . But where is she? How does she feel? Most importantly, what is she wearing?

One girl stood out amidst the crowd. She was not nervously pacing about like the others. Instead, she stood quietly and was perfectly still with her head slightly bowed. The girl took deep breaths. She was dressed in colorful leggings and a long, flowing skirt. A pair of sandals graced her feet. Her long, golden hair, laced with iridescent, sparkling ribbons, fell perfectly around her angelic face like a halo. This was the most important day of her entire life.

I'm nervous just thinking about it!

"Star Arianna—you're up next!" called a booming voice.

The man's voice echoed boldly throughout the auditorium. The girl slowly looked up, almost in disbelief. Did they really call her name? Her heart began to beat heavily in her chest. She stood frozen. A rush of chills pulsed through her body from the top of her head down to her feet. This was her defining moment!

The girl took a deep breath and lifted her shoulders. She forced herself to take a step, and then another. Her legs felt heavy like lead. As she moved through the crowd, she could hear their hushed voices: "She must be Star" . . . "Good luck, girl" . . . "Look at her leotard" . . . "Break a leg!" But with each step her stride grew lighter and her fear began to disappear. At the edge of the stage she stopped. Poised and ready to shine, she took a moment to whisper a prayer to Heaven. Then she lifted her chin, stood tall, and walked out onto the empty stage.

I'm doing it! I'm really writing a story about Star at her very first audition! I can't believe it. Thank You, Lord!

Chapter
Nine

"M-o-m! You *won't* believe it! I can hardly believe it!" Minutes later, Bridget went running from her bedroom in search of her mother. She was clutching her writing notebook tightly. "Mom? Where are you?" Bridget poked her head into the bonus room. It was empty. She ran downstairs into the kitchen. "Mom?"

"I'm outside, Bridget!" There was concern in Sandra Rhodes' voice as it wafted in from the screen door. "Are you okay?" she asked, her voice a bit louder.

Bridget didn't waste a second. She ran out the back door but suddenly collided with something. A spray of green beans and tomatoes spilled onto the patio. Bridget tripped backward, lost her footing on a tomato, and slipped to the ground. "Ouch!" she yelped, looking up. Her mother was standing over her with a basket partially full of vegetables from the garden.

"What on earth? Are you okay?" her mother gasped.

"I think so . . ." Bridget began pulling herself up. She felt a stinging pain in the palms of her hands. "I scraped my hands on the patio, but I think I'm okay."

"You ran right into me. Didn't you see me coming?" asked Mrs. Rhodes as she helped her daughter up and examined her hands. Bridget winced at the burning sensation.

"I didn't see you, Mom."

"Is something wrong? Is that why you came rushing out?" Mrs. Rhodes quickly asked.

"No. I was just so excited to tell you something wonderful," Bridget said, picking up her notebook.

"Let's get you inside and clean your hands and then you can tell me all about it," Mrs. Rhodes replied as they began walking into the house.

"Bridgey! Your legs are bleeding real bad!" shrieked Allison, who had just come running up onto the patio.

Startled, Mrs. Rhodes looked down at Bridget's legs and a broad smile broke across her face. "It's smooshed tomatoes, dear," she said to Allison. "Your sister is going to be just fine."

⊚ ⊚ ⊚

The rest of the early afternoon passed without incident. Bridget's hands were cleaned and bandaged. "Your scrapes are minimal," Mrs. Rhodes said thankfully. "Nothing a few bandages and antiseptic won't heal."

Bridget was truly glad. "I was worried that I wouldn't be able to write," she said.

"Yes—your story. Why don't you read it to Ali and me over lunch?" her mom suggested.

Bridget was thrilled with the idea. The three of them prepared lunch and took it out onto the newly cleaned patio. After they ate, Bridget sat Star in the middle of the table and cleared her throat. She opened up her notebook and began reading Star's story.

"One bright spotlight pooled in the center of a dark, empty stage," Bridget began. Mrs. Rhodes and Allison listened intently as Bridget's story unfolded.

"At the edge of the stage she stopped," Bridget continued. "Poised and ready to shine, she took a moment to whisper a prayer to Heaven. Then she lifted her chin, stood tall, and walked out onto the empty stage."

"'What will you be performing for us?' asked the director."

"'Climb Every Mountain from *The Sound of Music,*' Star Arianna said with confidence."

"'Go ahead,' the director stated. Star nodded and took another deep breath. Then she opened her mouth and began to sing—her clear, lovely voice echoing throughout the theater."

"Excellent!" her mother said, truly delighted at her daughter's creativity.

"I think it might be the best-est story I've ever heard!" Allison added.

"Thanks, Ali, but it's not quite done, yet," Bridget said with a giggle. Allison blushed sweetly.

"Do you think Auntie Faith will like it?" Bridget asked excitedly.

"Oh, I'm certain she'll like it very much," replied Mrs. Rhodes. "And speaking of Aunt Faith, I forgot to tell you that she called last night. You won't *believe* what my little sister has gone and done now," she said, popping a grape into her mouth and raising her eyebrows mischievously.

 Chapter
Ten

"Tell us, Mom!" Bridget pleaded, her pulse quickening. There was no one in the world whom Bridget admired more than her Aunt Faith. Bridget considered her the hippest, prettiest, smartest, and kindest person she knew, and Bridget wanted to be just like her.

"Well," her mother said, "several months ago the church that Faith joined in New York City began supporting a charity." Bridget listened curiously. "When your Aunt Faith heard about it from her pastor, she immediately got involved."

"That sure sounds like Auntie Faith—she's always volunteering for things. But what's the big news?" Bridget asked. She picked up Star and fiddled with the doll's clothes and hair.

"The big news is that the charity is an organization called 'Coiffure for Kids,'" Mrs. Rhodes replied.

Allison's round eyes grew bigger. "What's qua-foor?" she asked.

Bridget nodded. "Yeah, what's that mean?"

"It means that your Aunt Faith has cut her hair!" Mrs. Rhodes declared.

Allison and Bridget gasped. "Why, Mom? Why would Auntie Faith do such a thing?"

Bridget's eyes filled with tears. *Aunt Faith has—had—the longest, most beautiful hair of anyone I've ever known! She inspired me to grow my hair. How could she do this?* Bridget reached for her own long locks.

"*Coiffure* is a French word for *hairstyle,*" Mrs. Rhodes explained. "'Coiffure for Kids' is an organization that provides hairpieces for children who have lost their hair due to cancer or other diseases and can't afford a quality wig. Generous people, like your Aunt Faith, grow their hair long. Then they cut it and donate it to the charity. It's a very wonderful thing—what your aunt did," said Mrs. Rhodes tenderly.

Bridget swallowed hard. "Cut her hair? Is she okay?" she asked with exaggerated worry.

"Of course, she's fine," her mom replied. "There are more important things in life than hair," she said softly. "Aunt Faith made a personal sacrifice, and now another child will be blessed. Her sacrifice and generosity are a reflection of her inner beauty," said Mrs. Rhodes.

Bridget was letting it all sink in. *The last time I saw Auntie Faith we had such fun braiding and styling each other's hair.*

"Promise you'll never cut off your hair, Bridgey," said Allison with concern. "You're gonna have the longest hair in the sixth grade, remember?"

Bridget's mind was in a daze. "Longest what?" she muttered. "I'd never be that brave," she confessed in a near-whisper. "I've worked so hard and waited so long to grow mine out. Once it's gone, you can't put it back!"

Mrs. Rhodes smiled softly. She knew how much Bridget cared for her hair. She slowly stood and walked behind her daughter. Gently, she caressed Bridget's tendrils. "No one is asking you to cut your hair, darling," she said reassuringly. "That would be a true challenge," she said wistfully. "A true challenge, indeed."

 Chapter
Eleven

Bridget's Blog

In less than 24 hours I will board an airplane and soar through the sky—only to land upon the runway of my wildest dreams—New York City! It is really happening. 5ᵗʰ Avenue, here I come! (Auntie Faith, I can't wait to see your new haircut!)

NEWS FLASH!!!

I will be unveiling my masterpiece—Star's story—at, get this, a dramatic reading "open-mic" night at the Nervous Squirrel! Mrs. Hirsch emailed all of her students. She is organizing the event for the new sixth grade students who want to share the essays and stories they've written over the summer! It is scheduled for the Monday evening before the first day of school. The students who participate will get triple credit. You are all invited to attend. Pray for me, because I am already feeling very nervous about reading my story in public! I'll be facing the very challenge I blogged about!

Bridget finished her weekly blog entry and snapped the laptop shut.

"How soon until we leave?" she asked her mom, who was chopping up veggies.

Mrs. Rhodes glanced at the clock on the stove. "In twenty minutes. That will give me plenty of time to drop you off at the coffee shop before Ali's dental appointment," she said.

Bridget called Tina, and the girls made plans to meet. It would be their last visit together before Bridget left for New York City. "Oh, and Tina, don't forget the skirt," Bridget reminded her friend before hanging up.

The
Nervous Squirrel
Presents:

6th Grade Reading
Open-Mic Night!

"Did you see the poster on the door?" Tina asked, referring to the upcoming "open-mic" night.

Bridget walked over to Tina, who was already sitting at their favorite table in the window. "Yes! I can't believe it," Bridget said with a rush of emotion. "I'm going to do it for the extra credit, but I know I'll have awful stage fright. Are you going to share your essay?" asked Bridget.

"Sure! I'll do just about anything for extra credit in English. You know it's my weakest subject," Tina said. The girls placed their order and chatted about Tina's essay, which was entitled, "The Drop-Off Challenge."

"Thanks to your 'challenge blog,' Bridg, I now have some material to write about!" Tina quipped.

"It was your brilliant idea to begin with," Bridget reminded her friend.

"Anyway, I can't believe school is only two weeks away," Tina said between sips of a frozen caramel delight. Bridget felt butterflies in her stomach at the thought of starting the sixth grade. "Summer sure has gone by fast," Tina said. "I can't believe I've already been to the Grand Canyon and back."

"I know. And speaking of your vacation," Bridget said, "you've *got* to enter your pictures of the Grand Canyon into the photography contest this year. They are amazing! You're really a great photographer. Maybe you should join the yearbook staff," Bridget added.

Tina smiled. "Thanks, Bridg! Maybe I will."

"You must!" Bridget teased. "But you're right. Being so busy this summer sure has made the time go quickly." Bridget thought back to the first day of summer—writing her blog—penning her first short story—attending family gatherings—traveling to her grandparents' home in Michigan for their Fourth of July vacation—and their day trip to Pierce's Pike, among other things.

"I've been waiting all summer for this trip to New York City. It seems like it's taken forever to arrive. But now that it's here, everything's at high speed," Bridget said. Tina nodded in emphatic agreement. "I mean, tomorrow I leave for New York," Bridget continued, "then the day after I get back it's the open-mic night, and then school starts that following week," Bridget said theatrically. "It's all so overwhelming!" she declared.

Tina patted her friend on the arm. "Yeah, but at least you'll start the sixth grade with a whole new look," Tina said consolingly. Bridget gave her friend a questioning glance.

"Just imagine the stylish wardrobe you'll come home with from New York, silly!" exclaimed Tina.

Bridget grinned from ear to ear.

Chapter Twelve

Bridget stood at the Des Moines airport with her backpack in one hand and her purse in the other. Not only was it her first visit to New York City, it was also her first time on an airplane. But her excitement at seeing the famous city covered up any nerves she felt about flying.

"You take care of your mother, Bridget," her dad said with mock seriousness. "Don't let her get lost," he teased.

Sandra Rhodes rolled her eyes and elbowed her husband in the side. "That was a one-time thing," Sandra laughed, referring to the time she got lost on their honeymoon in Italy.

The Rhodes family said their good-byes, and Bridget and her mom boarded the plane. It was to be a seven-hour flight, including a layover in Houston to change planes. Bridget had a window seat and amused herself with the goings-on outside. She had Star right at her side to experience the journey with her. Together they watched as Bridget's pink leopard print suitcase was loaded onto the plane. "I can't believe it, Mom," Bridget said dreamily. "Thank you so much for doing this. My dreams are coming true."

Mrs. Rhodes smiled lovingly at her daughter. "I'm glad that we get to share in this together," she said.

☺ ☺ ☺

It was nearing 8:00 p.m. when the pilot announced that they were approaching New York's LaGuardia Airport. Bridget roused from a catnap and pressed her nose against the window. She caught her breath in her throat—the city was in full view, and it was more thrilling than anything she'd ever seen. The enormous buildings, pulsing lights, and moving traffic glowed and danced against the backdrop of a dimming summer night. Bridget couldn't speak. She quickly looked at her mother, pointed out the window, and then stared wide-eyed at the city below.

Before long they had exited the plane and gathered their luggage. As they made their way to the terminal, they scanned the crowd for signs of Faith. "I don't see her, Mom, do you?" Bridget asked.

"Hmmm, maybe she got stuck in traffic," Mrs. Rhodes said. "Let's go stand over there and keep an eye out for her."

Bridget and her mom made their way through a large group of people. A flash of color caught Bridget's attention. She peered through the crowd to see what it was, and then a shout escaped her lips. "Auntie Faith! Is that really you?"

A young woman in her late twenties emerged from the sea of people. She was dressed in a bright pink T-shirt and a long, funky skirt. A pair of stylish walking sandals graced her feet. But most striking was Faith's hair—a short, choppy pixie cut that made her blue eyes seem even larger and her cheekbones more prominent than ever.

"I can't believe it!" Bridget said breathlessly. "You look so different."

Aunt Faith flashed a dazzling smile and gave them both big hugs. "Welcome to New York!" she declared.

"But we must hurry—I've got a taxi waiting for us, and the meter's running!"

I wonder what her friends think of her hair, Bridget thought. *I'm still not sure what I think . . .*

In a flurry of excitement, Bridget and Sandra followed an assertive Faith through the crowd and outside to a big yellow taxi.

Bridget slid into the shiny cab, completely swept up in her first New York moment. "Just like on TV!" she said, her eyes wide with wonder.

"Driver, Christie's Deli in SoHo, please," Aunt Faith instructed. She sat back and smiled broadly at Bridget and Sandra, who were on either side of her. "In New York, it's not only possible but fashionable to have dinner after 9 p.m.!" she exclaimed. "You've simply *got* to try the brisket on rye and New York cheesecake!"

Bridget thought she would faint from euphoria.

Chapter Thirteen

The next evening, Bridget stepped out of the Minskoff Theater and onto 45th Street. It was the end of her first full day in the city. Her mind was awhirl. "I feel like I'm floating," she said to her aunt and mother. "I feel so—so—overwhelmed. *The Lion King* was the most amazing thing I've ever seen," she said, chattering with excitement. "My first full day in the Big Apple has totally outshined my wildest imagination!" Bridget gushed. Mrs. Rhodes nodded in agreement.

Aunt Faith threw her arm around her young niece. "I'm so glad you're enjoying yourself, Bridget!" she said. "It's fun to have you here." They began to walk through the theater district.

"Oh! Wait!" Bridget exclaimed. "Will you take my picture with Star in front of the theater?" she asked, taking the doll from her backpack purse. "It's part of *her* dream to be here, too," she said, "and I can show the photo at my public reading."

Star and Bridget posed in front of the theater with Tony Award–winning smiles. "I can't wait for you to read my story, Auntie Faith," Bridget said coyly. "I'd really like your professional opinion."

Faith hugged Bridget close. "I can't wait to read it! Your doll is fabulous—I'm sure she'll have a fabulous story."

They walked for a long time talking, recapping the day's events, and taking in the sights. Their first full day in the city had been invigorating. They used the subway system to get around, and Bridget was impressed with her aunt, who was a whiz at it. That morning after breakfast, Faith had taken them to the Metropolitan Museum of Art, where they had spent much of the morning and early afternoon exploring the beautiful artwork. Then they'd made their way to Herald Square for shopping and lunch at Macy's department store. Bridget was thrilled with the two new skirts, several shirts, and new pair of shoes that her stylish aunt helped her to pick out. "You'll look like a true New Yorker back in Wishing with these new clothes, Bridg," her aunt had said, and Bridget swelled at her fashionable aunt's approval. Then, after refreshing themselves back at Faith's apartment, they had topped off the day by seeing the award-winning musical *The Lion King*.

"Ladies, would you like a late-night snack?" Aunt Faith asked after nearly an hour of walking.

"Yes!" Bridget and her mom sang in unison.

They made their way to Carnegie Deli on 7th Avenue, where Bridget was awestruck with the pickles and dangling sausages behind the meat counter. But what really caught her eye was the refrigerated cake carousel that displayed a dozen or more of the most decadent cakes and desserts she had ever seen. "I'll take a slice of *that*," Bridget said wide-eyed, pointing to a larger-than-life pie rotating in the carousel. "What is it?" she asked the waitress bashfully.

"That's our Hershey's Fifth Avenue Bavarian Chocolate Cream Pie," the waitress stated, a little too loudly in Bridget's opinion. Bridget blushed. She was even more embarrassed when the waitress presented her with an enormous slice of the pie. But Bridget made no apologies when she finished every mouth-watering bite.

# Chapter
Fourteen

Bridget's Blog: Live from New York City!

It's well past midnight in "the city
that never sleeps," and guess what? I
can't sleep! I'm on a high from our
first day here (and probably from the
huge slice of pie I ate an hour ago!).
I had to take a moment to write and
tell everyone how much fun I am having.
Tomorrow Aunt Faith is taking us to
her church, and after that we will go
see her office building. Then she is
taking us to some "non-touristy" sites
(as she calls them) so that we can

experience life in New York like true natives. Should be fun . . .

Bridget finished her blog on Faith's sleek laptop and looked over at her mom, who was fast asleep on Faith's pull-out sofa bed. Bridget walked over to the living room window and took one last look out onto the never-ending city. *Sure is nothing like the Thompsons' grain silo*, Bridget thought romantically. *Lord, I don't know how to thank You for this experience*, she prayed. Then exhaustion finally hit and she crawled into bed next to her mom.

☉ ☉ ☉

"I'm *very* impressed, Bridget!"

Aunt Faith and Bridget sat at Faith's tiny kitchen table munching on fresh fruit and hearty New York bagels. Bridget had just shared her short story with her aunt over breakfast while her mom showered.

"You really made your doll come to life! That's a mark of a good writer," Aunt Faith said. "Your descriptions are wonderful! I felt like I was backstage watching the whole audition," she added. Bridget was truly surprised at her aunt's positive feedback.

"You're a special young lady," Faith said after a few moments, looking Bridget in the eyes. "I know God has a very unique plan for your life."

Bridget's cheeks flushed. She held Star tightly in her hands and looked down at the doll—her aunt's encouraging words penetrating deep into her heart.

"Your blog is also a real encouragement to me," Faith said. "I anticipate reading it each week."

Bridget looked up in surprise. "Really?" she asked.

"Really!" Faith said with a warm smile. "It keeps the family connected and allows us to share in each other's faith."

"But *you* inspire me," Bridget said. "Like cutting off your hair. I can't stop thinking about it. I know it was for a good cause, but weren't you scared?" she asked.

"It was hard to part with my hair," Faith admitted. "But the reward was greater, and that's why I did it. When we sacrifice something precious to us, the Lord gives back a blessing so intense that it's almost too much to contain," she said with mounting enthusiasm.

Bridget was getting excited, too. Her aunt's joy was contagious. *Joy in sacrifice*—Bridget thought to herself with much interest—*Are You trying to teach me something important, Lord?*

"Let me show you what I mean," Faith said. She got up and rummaged through a large basket of books and magazines. Then she handed Bridget a little photo album. The front of the album was colorfully hand-decoupaged.

"These are my friends," Faith said.

Bridget opened the album. Her heart stung at the first picture. It was a little girl, about the same age as Allison, sitting in a hospital bed. The girl had a beaming smile, but she was completely bald.

"Her name is Rachel," Aunt Faith said. "She's the same age as Ali. She had cancer, and the chemotherapy made her lose all of her hair," she explained. "But turn the page," Aunt Faith said excitedly.

Bridget turned the page. "Wow!" she exclaimed. "Is that—"

"Yes," Aunt Faith said. "That's her." The picture showed the same little girl—only she had beautiful, long blonde hair. "It was so touching when she got her wig," Faith said.

"Oh, Auntie Faith," Bridget began, her eyes welling with tears, "this is so wonderful. I can see why you got involved."

What a special gift to give to someone in need, Bridget thought to herself. *What an extraordinary sacrifice . . .*

"Is she still sick?" Bridget asked through tears.

"No," Faith said, "she's in recovery. The cancer has been successfully destroyed."

Bridget flipped through the photo album. There were more pictures of her aunt with children in the hospital.

"I try to visit the hospital a few times a month," Aunt Faith shared. "The children are very dear to my heart," she said. "So you see, the sacrifice of cutting my hair has given me greater joy—knowing that a child will have a wig of her very own."

Bridget's heart was filled with great admiration for her aunt. "You seem like a whole new person," Bridget said softly, seeing her aunt in a different light, "and not just because your hair is shorter," she quickly added.

Aunt Faith smiled. "I've learned a lot this past year," she said. "A lot about what is important in life. The Lord brought 'Coiffure for Kids' across my path, and I knew I had to get involved. Not only did I donate my hair, but now I donate my time as a volunteer. Many more children are in need of quality wigs, and I help to raise awareness in businesses throughout the city. I also visit sick children in the hospitals, and they've changed my life," Faith said. "The children and their families are very brave," she said, her voice quivering with a rush of emotion.

"And besides that," she said, regaining her composure with a fresh burst of energy, "making the move to such a large city has caused me to step out of my comfort zone and really rely on God. Like in your blog—you'll be moving to a bigger school and that will cause you to rely on God more, too," she said.

"I guess you could say that I've grown up some,"

Faith mused, running her fingers through her short tresses.

Bridget thought about her aunt's words. They sat in silence for a few moments before Faith spoke up.

"So do you like New York so far?" she asked her niece. "There are so many places to see and fun things to do here," Aunt Faith continued. "Is there anything special you'd like to do today?"

Bridget thought about it for a split second and then replied, "There *is* something I'd really like to do before I leave this amazing city."

"Just name it!" Aunt Faith declared before taking a big bite of a sesame bagel.

Chapter Fifteen

ridget! Are you ready?" Michael Rhodes called upstairs to his daughter.

It was early evening on the day after she returned home from her trip to the Big Apple. Bridget stood in front of the bathroom mirror. She took a deep breath. "Coming," she replied.

She slowly made her way down the stairs and was surprised to see her dad, mom, and sister waiting for her at the bottom of the steps. "This is for you," her dad said, handing her a little wrapped box. Bridget was taken aback. "We're really proud of all you've accomplished these last couple of months," he said, "and we wanted to give you something special as a memento of your summer." Bridget was deeply touched by her father's affirmation.

"You've grown up quite a bit this summer, dear," her mom added. "We're so pleased with the wonderful young woman you are becoming."

Allison, who was cute as ever in her "I Love New York" ball cap that Bridget had bought for her, ran over and gave her sister a hug. "I love you, Bridgey," she said sweetly.

"I don't know what to say," Bridget said, her eyes misty.

"Then why not open your present?" Allison asked, matter-of-factly. The family giggled.

"Great idea, Ali," Bridget agreed. She tugged at the fine ribbon on the package and gently unsheathed the smooth, thick wrapping until she held a white box in her hands. A golden seal wrapped around the box. The inscription read *Metropolitan Museum of Art*. Bridget glanced up at her mother, who smiled knowingly. Bridget carefully broke the seal and opened the lid. There before her was a glittering star pendant. Bridget gasped.

"I bought it while we were at the museum," her mother said. "Your Aunt Faith said that it is truly an expression of who you are."

"It's amazing!" Bridget exclaimed in awe.

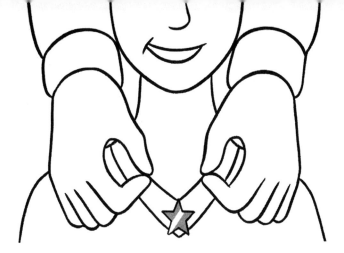

"A special necklace for a very special young lady," her dad said tenderly as he helped to fasten it around Bridget's neck. "Very, very beautiful," he said, standing back and looking into his daughter's eyes.

"I love it! Thank you!" Bridget exclaimed.

"I know you've been anxious all summer about starting middle school," her mom said. "Let this necklace remind you to shine the light of God in all you do. Matthew 5:16 says, 'Let your light shine before men, that they may see your good deeds and praise your Father in heaven.' People will be drawn to your kindness and good deeds more than any outfit or hairstyle you could wear."

Bridget's gleaming necklace was the perfect accessory to her shining smile.

The Rhodes family pulled into the parking lot of the Nervous Squirrel. *Looks like I'm the nervous squirrel tonight,* Bridget thought. *I've really got the jitters. What if I get up in front of that crowd and can't speak a single word?*

Bridget grasped her manuscript with one hand and gently touched her necklace with the other. Star Arianna, who began the summer's journey with her, sat on her lap. Bridget was filled with anticipation. She could see that the coffeehouse was crowded with students—some faces familiar, and some new.

"I guess this is it," she whispered to Star.

Bridget got out of the car and smoothed her new skirt. Michael Rhodes led the way into the shop. It was bustling with people and voices. Bridget paused and took a deep, calming breath before she stepped inside. Poised and ready to shine, she took a moment to whisper a prayer to Heaven. Then she lifted her chin, stood tall, and walked into the crowded shop.

"You *really* did it!" A girl's voice rose above the buzz of the crowd. It was Emily Daniels. Tina was in tow. "Tina made me promise I wouldn't tell! I can't believe it, Bridget!"

86

Tina motioned to Bridget's sparkling necklace, winked, and mouthed the words, "bling bling!" Bridget nodded her head in agreement.

Before she knew what was happening, a crowd of friends from school, many of whom Bridget hadn't seen very often over the summer, gathered around her.

"New York really made its impression on you," one boy teased.

"I would never be that brave," another girl quipped.

"You seem like a whole new person," Emily declared.

Tina moved closer and squeezed Bridget's shoulder.

Bridget couldn't help but smile nervously at all the attention. "Thanks," she said earnestly, running her fingers through her new short, choppy pixie cut.

"I guess you could say I've grown up some," she added, quoting a well-admired source.

Chapter Sixteen

Star Arianna stood on the stage—but this time it was not empty. The auditions were completed. The singers and actors gathered nervously on the stage and waited for the director to announce who won the lead roles in the upcoming Broadway musical.

" 'I have great news,' the director announced. 'Each person standing on this stage will have a part in the musical.'

"The group erupted in cheers, and Star herself clapped and felt a wave of relief. She was simply thrilled to be a part of the production.

" 'We have need for a large chorus,' the director explained, 'but as you know, only two people can hold the lead roles. So without any more delay, I'd like to announce the lead cast members.'

"The room became quiet once again. Star's pulse quickened.

" 'For the male lead role, I'd like to congratulate Joseph Marson. Joseph, please step forward and present yourself to the cast.'

"From the middle of the group a tall, young man stepped to the front of the stage. His face was beaming with excitement. The crowd cheered. Then the director spoke again.

" 'And now, for the lead female role, I'd like to congratulate a very talented and brave newcomer—her name is—Star Arianna. Star, please come forward.'

"Star couldn't believe her ears! Her dream had come true! With a prayer of thanks in her heart, she stepped forward through the cheering crowd."

◎ ◎ ◎

Bridget finished reading her short story and looked up hesitantly at the faces in the crowded coffee shop. There was an intimidating moment of silence before the group of students and family erupted in applause.

I did it! I got through the reading! Bridget smiled broadly. It was a wonderful moment of relief and exhilaration.

"Thank you so much," she said. "I'd like to say one more thing," Bridget began as the room grew quiet.

"As many of you have noticed, I cut my hair this summer while I was in New York City visiting my Aunt Faith." Many familiar faces smiled and nodded at her.

"My Aunt Faith introduced me to her friends — friends who are children, some even our age," she said, pointing to her classmates. "But her friends have cancer, and they have lost their hair due to their medical treatments. When my aunt told me about it, I was really challenged. You see, I had long hair. It took me years to grow it out. In fact, my goal at the beginning of summer was to have the longest hair in the sixth grade. But when I saw the pictures of the children in the hospital, I felt in my heart that I needed to get involved. You can't imagine how tough it was to cut off my hair. I did it with God's help," Bridget said. "And now another little girl in recovery will have a stylish wig to wear while her own hair grows out."

Spontaneous cheers broke out in the little coffee shop.

"My aunt and her church showed me that my small sacrifice can mean a lot to another person who has need. There are a lot of ways we can all help. The children need more than just new hair. Some have few or no friends to visit them or cheer them up. We can be involved right here in our own community by sending the kids cards, books to read, pajamas, or even a doll to keep them company. We can each be a part of their healing and treatment.

"If any of you are interested in donating your hair or your time to 'Coiffure for Kids' or to other charities, please let me know after this event. I can tell you more about it and the kids that it will help. Thanks for listening!"

The group gave Bridget a standing ovation. Bridget was stunned and elated as she walked back to her seat.

Lord—this must be the joy Auntie Faith was talking about—the joy of sacrifice!

☼ Chapter Seventeen

Bridget's Blog

It's the last official day of summer! Time has flown by these past three months. So much has happened over the summer. I'm grateful for all of my experiences . . . I can't believe school starts tomorrow. I'm so excited even though the butterflies in my stomach are really fluttering! I have my outfit all picked out—brand-new skirt, blouse, and shoes from New York (thanks to Auntie Faith for being my personal shopper!). But my best accessory is what I carry inside of me. I'm going to let my light shine! I won't be starting school with the longest hair in my class (for some silly reason I thought that it would help me fit in), but I plan on shining God's light the brightest and having lots of fun along the way!

Even though summer is coming to an end, I'm anticipating a new beginning. So I'm happy to announce that my summer blog will turn into the musings of a sixth grade trendsetter who is on the move with God! Be sure to check out my blog weekly for the latest in sixth grade fun, faith, and fashion. I'm sure there will be plenty of drama to write about. Remember it's F.Y.E.O.

Oh, and if you're wondering about Star Arianna, she went on to win a Tony Award for her Broadway performance. She's fearlessly pursuing the theater in New York and she now regularly donates her time to helping kids with cancer.

Bridget—signing off . . . to catch up on her beauty sleep in preparation for her big debut on the sixth grade stage. I'll keep you posted!